ISAKO
ISAKO

ISAKO ISAKO

Mia Ayumi Malhotra

Alice James Books
Farmington, Maine
www.alicejamesbooks.org

10 9 8 7 6 5 4 3 2 1

Alice James Books are published by Alice James Poetry Cooperative, Inc., an affiliate of the University of Maine at
Farmington.

Alice James Books
114 Prescott Street
Farmington, ME 04938
www.alicejamesbooks.org

Library of Congress Cataloging-in-Publication Data

Names: Malhotra, Mia Ayumi, author.
Title: Isako Isako / Mia Ayumi Malhotra.
Description: Farmington, ME : Alice James Books, 2018.
Identifiers: LCCN 2018020533 (print) | LCCN 2018021443 (ebook) | ISBN
    9781948579506 (eBook) | ISBN 9781938584947 (pbk. : alk. paper)
Subjects: LCSH: Japanese Americans--Fiction.
Classification: LCC PS3613.A4356 (ebook) | LCC PS3613.A4356 I83 2018 (print)
    | DDC 813/.6--dc23
LC record available at https://lccn.loc.gov/2018020533

Alice James Books gratefully acknowledges support from individual donors, private foundations, the University of Maine at
Farmington, the National Endowment for the Arts, and the Amazon Literary Partnership.

ART WORKS.
arts.gov

amazon literary
partnership

Cover image: "Thinking of the Sun" by Louise Kukuchi

Contents

Part II: A History of Lost Things

Part III: In the Quiet after

Acknowledgments

Grateful acknowledgment is made to the journals in which versions of these poems first appeared:

Asian American Literary Review, "Crossing," "The Kind of Morning"

Bone Bouquet, "A History of Isako" (section III), "Another History of Isako" (section II)

Cimarron Review, "Cebu"

The Collagist, "Another History of Isako" (section III, as "[My grandmother is dying]")

Connotation Press: An Online Artifact, "Portrait of Isako in Wartime," "Polytrauma"

Cutbank, "Bathing Isako" (as "Mother at Bath")

DIAGRAM, "Portrait in Sickness and Health" (as "[A mechanical beeping fills the space]")

Diode, "Isako Shows Her Daughter How to Ply the Line" (as "He shows the child how to ply the line"), "A History of Isako" (sections I and II, as "A History of Grandmother")

Drunken Boat, "The Street Where a Certain Democratic Leader Lives" (section II), "Another History of Isako" (section I, as "A History of Isako")

Fogged Clarity, "Self-Portrait as Sparrows and Blood," "Lost Things I" (as "Isako, Lost Things I)

The Fourth River, "After Hiroshima," "Isako's Rules to Remember"

The Greensboro Review, "Salmon Song: Migration" (as "The Locks")

Hyphen, "To My Many Mothers, Issei and Nisei," "One Day You'll Look in the Mirror and See Lions"

inter|rupture, "Elegy for the Unborn" (as "Lenora")

Kartika Review, "Scenes from a Childhood"

The Monarch Review, "As If," "Sunday in Skagit Valley"

Pacifica Literary Review, "Late Pantoum: Isako, Illness" (as "Someday")

They Will Sew the Blue Sail, "The Street Where a Certain Democratic Leader Lives" (section I)

Tinderbox Poetry Journal, "City of Sandalwood"

wildness, "At the Cliff House" (as "Land's End") and "The Losing Begins" (as "The End When It Comes")

Witness, "Isako, Last Spring" (as "Isako Isako"), "A Last History of Isako," "[Without Isako]," "Isako like Ash Your Sister Drifts Back to You"

I would like to thank Carey Salerno, Alyssa Neptune, and the wonderful staff at Alice James Books for bringing this book into being. Thanks also to the Kundiman family, Vandana Khanna, Kenji C. Liu, Maria Hummel, Pimone Triplett, Andrew Feld, Linda Bierds, M. NourbeSe Philip, and Paul Sakai for their support and invaluable input. A special note of gratitude to my family, especially Mark Malhotra, for always believing.

for

Shigeko Tabuchi Sakai
(1923–2010)

and

Sachiko Iwai Higaki
(1924–2017)

We are linked to one another's bodies, throughout time and history, in a female lineage that has carried on the human story, carried the men and the women, given life and suck to all the living, closed the eyes of all the dead.

—*Naomi Ruth Lowinsky*

To My Many Mothers, Issei and Nisei

Praise be to beef liver stew, to gravy biscuits
      and home-baked bread, to women
in work pants and suspenders who *worked like dogs*
      in the packing shed, up to elbows
in rose clippings. You fed us well, O goddesses
      of goulash and green beans, of Sunday dinners
wrangled from the coop. For penny money
      and seamstressing, praise. For parsnips
and sweet potatoes, praise. Even for the years lost
      to sharecropping and strawberries, hallelujah.
You worked until the final hour then rose
      three days later, baby squalling on your hip,
back to breaking canes, clipping hooks,
      hustling the men through lunch hour.
No breaks, boys. Hallelujah to Pond's Cold Cream,
      to curling rags and church bento socials.
Praise to the nursery truck revving in the morning,
      the clank of steel pipes and boiler-
house rumble. All glory to the Berkeley streetcar
      and Key Route electric train, the smokestacks
of Richmond and foggy peaks of San Francisco.
      And because they're what taught us to praise,
glory to the roses run wild, the packing shed
      left to cobweb. Praise to the crowded horse stalls

and half-built barracks of Rohwer, Arkansas,

   dusty sheets and muffled nights of Block 9-9-C,

100. *Sakai, Chu. 102. Sakai, Ruby. 103. Sakai, Kazue.*

   O praise to the camp midwives, the Nisei girls

shooting hoops and swatting birdies when their mothers

   weren't looking. And to the college-bound coed

who crossed the country, camp release papers

   in hand, hallelujah. Her truth marches on.

WESTERN DEFENSE COMMAND AND FOURTH ARMY
WARTIME CIVIL CONTROL ADMINSTRATION
Presidio of San Francisco, California
May 3, 1942

INSTRUCTIONS
TO ALL PERSONS OF
JAPANESE
ANCESTRY

Living in the Following Area:

All of that portion of the County of Alameda, State of California, within the boundary beginning at the point where the southerly limits of the City of Oakland meet San Franscico Bay; thence easterly and following the southerly limits of said city to U.S. Highway No. 50; thence southerly and easterly on said Highway No. 50 to its intersection with California State Highway No. 21; thence southerly on said Highway No. 21 to its intersection, at or near Warm Springs, with California State Highway No. 17; thence southerly on Highway No. 17 to the Alameda-Santa Clara County line; then westerly and following said county line to San Francisco Bay; then northerly, and following the shoreline of San Francisco Bay to the point of beginning.

Pursuant to the provisions of Civilian Exclusion Order No. 34, this Headquarters, dated May 3, 1942, all persons of Japanese ancestry, both alien and non-alien, will be evacuated from the above area by 12 o'clock noon, P.W.T., Saturday, May 9, 1942.

No Japanese person living in the above area will be permitted to change residence after 12 o'clock noon, P.W.T., Sunday, May 3, 1942, without obtaining special permission from the representative of the Commanding General, Northern California Sector, at the Civil Control Station located at:

920 - "C" Street,

Hayward, California.

Such permits will only be granted for the purpose of uniting members of a family, or in cases of grave emergency.

The Civil Control Station is equipped to assist the Japanese population affected by this evacuation in the following ways:

1. Give advice and instructions on the evacuation.

2. Provide services with respect to the management, leasing, sale, storage or other disposition of most kinds of property, such as real estate, business and professional equipment, household goods, boats, automobiles and livestock.

3. Provide temporary residence elsewhere for all Japanese family groups.

4. Transport persons and a limited amount of clothing and equipment to their new residence.

The Following Instructions Must Be Observed:

1. A responsible member of each family, preferably the head of the family, or the person in whose name most of the property is held, and each individual living alone, will report to the Civil Control Station to receive further instructions. This must be done between 8:00 A.M. and 5:00 P.M. on Monday, May 4, 1942, or between 8:00 A.M. and 5:00 P.M. on Tuesday, May 5, 1942.

2. Evacuees must carry with them on departure for the Assembly Center, the following property:

(a) Bedding and linens (no mattress) for each member of the family;

(b) Toilet articles for each member of the family;

(c) Extra clothing for each member of the family;

(d) Sufficient knives, forks, spoons, plates, bowls and cups for each member of the family;

(e) Essential personal effects for each member of the family.

4

All items carried will be securely packaged, tied and plainly marked with the name of the owner and numbered in accordance with instructions obtained at the Civil Control Station. The size and number of packages is limited to that which can be carried by the individual or family group.

3. No pets of any kind will be permitted.

4. No personal items and no personal goods will be shipped to the Assembly Center.

5. The United States Government through its agencies will provide for the storage, at the sole risk of the owner, of the more substantial household items, such as iceboxes, washing machines, pianos and other heavy furniture. Cooking utensils and other small items will be accepted for storage if crated, packed and plainly marked with the name and address of the owner. Only one name and address will be used by a given family.

6. Each family, and individual living alone, will be furnished transportation to the Assembly Center or will be authorized to travel by private automobile in a supervised group. All instructions pertaining to the movement will be obtained at the Civil Control Station.

**Go to the Civil Control Station
between the hours of 8:00 A.M. and 5:00 P.M.,
Monday, May 4, 1942,
or between the hours of 8:00 A.M. and 5:00 P.M.,
Tuesday, May 5, 1942,
to receive further instructions.**

J.L. DeWITT
Lieutenant General, U.S. Army
Commanding

SEE CIVILIAN EXCLUSION ORDER NO. **34**

A History of Isako

I.

During war Isako is lady watch city fade to rubble. Is lady hide in Kobe church as air raid siren shrill overhead. Is lady strain for voice of emperor on radio then sell kimono and shred boiled potato to rice. Is lady watch as shrapnel slice body like pickled ginger to be dyed pink and buried. Dip finger in saltwater then take rice in cupped palm. Press tightly and release. Is lady cross Pacific on S.S. Cleveland. Isako is lady turn from train track when spat upon. Is lady in Arkansas desert. Is lady wipe dust from tin plate in mess hall. Is released from camp to board Whites Only train. Is lady wipe spittle from cheek in Cincinnati and leave sorority. Mark difference. Isako is lady tape name to bottom of casserole dish before church potluck. Tuck blade beneath box spring next to No. 11 knitting needle. Behind barbed wire all question run to one.

II.

I do not remember where Isako is during the war. Is it Osaka or is it Ohio. I do not wish to appear foolish. There is the question of authenticity.

When I write about Isako I use words like _____ and _____ knowing such designations make no sense. I use these details to make Isako at home on a page that is otherwise white.

I put the rim of my teacup against my lip and blow to create a dampening effect.

I wish to write about this important person in my life but cannot do so without saying _____ or _____.

Instead I write about dust. A pigment that stains yellow and cannot be removed.

III.

I wear a kimono only once in my life. The garment once belonged to Isako although it has been hemmed twice and bears several discolorations on the bodice. I have no idea how to reassemble the garment and leave it poorly folded in its paper sleeve. Traditionally this knowledge is passed from mother to daughter. Isako scolds me for rumpling the collar then smoothes it along the traditional folds. A kimono tied right over left is a sign that the wearer is deceased. In English all words begin in the left margin and disappear into the right. I rewrap the garment believing a new grammar may be necessary.

IV.

instructions to all living persons Japanese in the following ancestry area persons alien will be evacuated pursuant to from non-alien ancestry noon provisions this dated 12 o'clock P.W.T. Saturday Commanding Executive Order No. 34 no persons will be permitted living no Japanese will be living to change residence area after 12 o'clock noon P.W.T. Saturday May 9, 1942 without obtaining permission the Commanding General Civil Control Station located permits will be granted such only for purpose the uniting members or family emergency grave in cases evacuees must carry property following them on departure for Assembly Center between hours the 8AM the 5PM bedding (no mattress) linens for members each of family articles toilet for members each of family will be packaged marked plainly with name and owner numbered in accordance

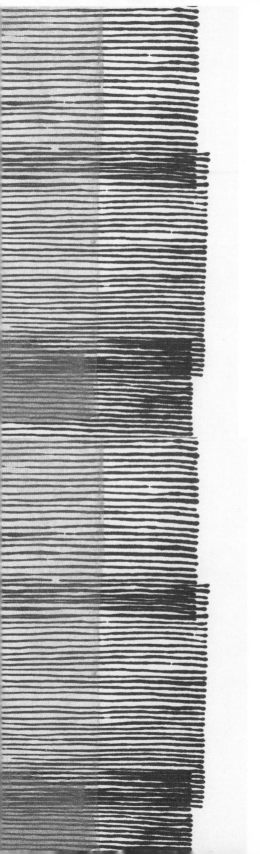

Part I: Legion My Lesion

Self-Portrait as Sparrows and Blood

For the price of a tooth, you can buy two from the boy with no legs. One to keep, the other to let. As in ancient times, the first slit over a bowl of fresh water, the second dipped into the blood of its twin. Water beading on the sheath of its beak. As a child, I observed the talons' delicate architecture. How bent, the weighted tendons snapped shut, clamping the toes in place. Even in sleep, a bird does not lose its perch. A sparrow found on the front steps sputters like a guttering flame when fed from an eyedropper. The tiny body is limp in my hand, cold in the ground where I lay it. So tiny you could crush its skull between two fingers. The *crunch* of wing bones as the pitted struts collapse. On the sidewalk, a bloodied wing, opened as if in flight. The rest of the bird, incomplete, hovering overhead. The curve of bone like a feathered cuff. *None of us escapes unscathed. None of us is free.* It's true what they say, that airborne, a bird's bones fill with flight. Set free in an open field, the bird thinking *why not me.* Blood smeared across keeled breastbone, bright against its throat. Each wingbeat a scarlet flash. The pressed-together parts mirrored in the bottom of the bowl. Halves opening outward like sky.

Scenes from a Childhood

(Vientiane, Laos)

I.

Memory runs along the border like a dark chain,
and I'm back on Platform 9, ticket in hand.
We settle into berths barely big enough for sleep,

losing light in degrees. The story dims,
and all I know narrows to a row of hooks
fixed to the curtain drawn across my seat.

Memory lurches, and a girl begins to scream,
wails rising from the ragged tear of her throat.
She's crazy, someone says. *Yaa baa.*

What did I feel that night, shrinking
from the bodies bulging against fabric
into my berth—and her, thrashing in the aisle?

The girl falls to pieces for reasons that fail me,
even now. Could be the adults knew. Or the boy
crouched over her, shadows moving like cuts

across his skin. How is it I can't remember her face
but recall the way the light looked as it deepened
to dusk? Blotchy patches of dark, screams from beyond

the curtain, scenery breaking apart. An overhead
bunk swings down, clicks into place. The mind works
to fix the details: which way the light switched *on*,

which way *off*. An unsteady rumble, the train swerves
left, right. A scuffle of voices; below, the rhythmic
ka-chunk ka-chunk of wheels along railroad ties.

II.

Tell me if I'm about to hit something,
        I said and closed my eyes, flew by
in a whir of chains nattering
        like teeth around metal sprockets.
Turn left, my friend said, and I threaded
        my handlebars into the turn—   *Straight*
and I steadied myself, pushed faster,
        farther into what felt like drifting
on delicate strings pulled by another.
        A moment so quick we nearly missed it,
split skin and blood, frontal bone
        crushed on the stairs' beveled edge.
What happened next, mother screaming
        on the other side, pulling at my wrists,
the curtain, crying, *You need stitches,*
        trying to reach the body I'd twisted
into yellow fabric. Her words came clear,
        Stay straight   as from the body I drifted.

III.

I had no rope, called, *Dog, dog*, as I wobbled
on my bike across rice paddies and irrigation
ditches, waited for the *pad-pad* of his paws,
tail loosened to a ready wag. *Dog, dog*,
on down the drive, past rows of bicycles
parked along the side of the house.

How many times have I halted memory's reel,
rewound the instant I reached the back steps,
rabbit cage coming into view. My cries, too late,
the rabbits' screams, unearthly, like a child's
but worse, a whistling in the throat.

Their bodies caught in chicken wire,
dog, dog and *stop, stop*. The quick whip
of his tail as he flashed by, matted fur,
scrabble of claws against concrete, and me,
falling after the body, the blunt *force* of it.

Afterward, I held the biggest one to my
chest, waited for the kicking to slow.
In its eyes, not blame but its
reflection. Two gold-ringed flares.

As If

this, my wish: to be cord-
shorn, wrapped in white.

My unwashed neck's been
rung with gold. As if this

were the god whose head
I wished to crown, the one

whose hem I wished myself
beneath. He rubbed my

wound with salt, stitched
me shut like lace. My wild

tongue whistles, I'm all in-
cisor & skull. Ruff-bitten,

tooth-cut, I rustle in my rude
warren, pluck fur from my

belly to line my nest. We,
the hunted, are formed to

flee, feet furred for speed.

City of Sandalwood

A city of remnants:
moss-covered, crumbling
stupas at every intersection.
A hair fallen from Buddha's
head, his passing footprints
preserved in stone. Mute, lost,
as though living underwater,
that's how we first arrived.

I still remember the world
blinded by noonday sun,
the slow gait of water buffalo
shambling down the road,
bellies crusted with mud.
How sunset lit the Mekong
on fire, kerosene poured
from a flame-colored sky.

Someday I'll go back to those
elegant, weary boulevards. Teak-
lined streets, buildings buckling .
under the weight of ruin, empire.
The grounds of my childhood
home, overrun with frangipani.

We vanished without a trace.
Handprints in concrete, a pair
of house sparrows buried
in the front yard. How little
we leave behind. Feathers
on the bottom of a birdcage,
a cat found dead in a pool
of spilled petrol. A trick
of childhood, how details elude,
even as they're remembered.

Early Pantoum: SFO International Airport, 1992

I buried my face in my hands
and left it there. When my body rose
to pass through customs gate,
life fell back to normal proportions,

and I left. When nobody rose
to follow us through, I sighed,
because life felt normal. Proportional:
mom, dad, brother. Our luggage

followed us through. I lost sight
of the relatives waving from the gate
at mom, dad, brother, our luggage.
I felt strangely unburdened

by the relatives waving. From the gate,
I turned for a final glance,
felt unburdened at last. The strangeness
of American supermarkets.

Turning, I took a final glance
at that unfamiliar world
of American supermarkets.
I was headed home, though

that too felt unfamiliar.
Soon I'd take on new customs,
headed home, though there too,
I'd have to bury my face.

A Decade Later, You Return to Your Childhood Home

No one knows the exact whereabouts
of the ovaries; some things we're not
meant to remember. After your mom

died, you left your childhood home
for good. Ten years later, it's intact
only in memory. We siphon slowly

through the city, watch the skyline
slide past. Crossing the Washington
Bridge, you've come home at last,

where some things we're not meant
to hold. Tumors are most frequently
found in the ovaries' epithelium.

Pressing hand to pelvic crest, I imagine
the incision, sutures. Steel instruments
easing each organ apart. Though this

is where we all began, no one wants
to return. Memory takes its retreat,
shuts the lights off, room by room.

Still, something stirs. Life's germ shifts
imperceptibly—the future, a tiny, single-
celled fact, a body humming with secrets.

Adenocarcinoma

Meaning: of the glands. From the Greek *karkinos*—
"crab growth." At certain stages the tumor resembles

a cauliflower. Not everything makes sense. Two bodies,
while sparring, create a set of interlocking fingers,

a spongy mass riddled with lesions. A desert of devastation.
There's something hidden in the hieroglyphs

of stranded bodies. They glint and stiffen
in the sun, a legion of bony-mouthed fish.

It's itchy, she says. *My body pinches.* I am a lost dot.
I would scale these heights for you, but I fear the depths.

Every day one trillion tons of water evaporate
from the world's oceans. To evaporate: to turn

to vapor. To disappear. You can close your mouth,
but somewhere else, another will open.

Another History of Isako

I.

Isako is lady hold hand to chest one morning say *chotto chotto dizzy.* Is lady short of breath which draws through straw with chewed out bottom. *Something tingly.* Is lady scratch in front of mirror *chotto itchy around tummy.* Is lady who looks on the internet for signs clicks through the stages 1 2 3 finally 4. Whose heart muddies. Is told not likely no we don't believe so. Is lady fit knife in base of belly pull fish open and filet. Is lady point to suji say *all this no good see this and this too.* Is lady pare meat from bones. Is filled with lesions doctors don't see at first. Is lady lie in bed organs pulled from chest cavity heart lungs and kidney. Is lady pressed to feathers on shiny black background. Is mass the size of a child's fist. Is lady branch to smaller and smaller divisions which end in clusters of alveoli. Is lady emptied. Is lady think *dear god   dear*

II.

The lungs at birth are pinkish-white but in time become mottled with black. *Take some apricots* Isako says. *Take more.* Tiny pitted fruit fall from her hands. Clumps of rosy flesh. The rush of juice on the tongue. Between mismatched lobes beat the heart's elegant arches. *Right here* Isako says. I watch as Isako reaches out and presses her shoulder blade. Tucked behind the vena cava lies the tumor's distressed surface. Shocking against the smooth interior of the lung. Did you know that as a child I ate so many apricots I was sick. The body mistakenly lodged in the windpipe. What I remember. The coughing the retching each cartilaginous ring contracting violently. Recanting every bite.

III.

The walls are white and angled outward though at first I attempt to move to the next piece
there is no escaping this odd architecture I turn and turn but the center is always there is
no turning back as I step closer to the painting what fills the vision large kidney-shaped
blotches like red blood cells black swirls which pull down the canvas like a window shade
tumors have spread between Isako's lungs they say into the lymphatic system this morning
Isako woke saying *something feels funny in my head* I do not believe this possible try to step
away from the painting its reds its black its dramatic fingers reaching from organs that bleed
in every direction this is not how the space is designed I am meant to face it head on there
is no turning back.

Isako like Ash Your Sister Drifts Back to You

During the war Isako you tell me your sister her daughters half-Japanese turned the neighbors cold this memory Isako a thicket that cannot be breached how it rises to block the sky nights Isako you tell me you darkened the windows readied a pot of uncooked rice for the pit in your front yard deep as a grave Isako out of the wanderings of history you have emerged Isako on this white couch all the body fallen from your bones to hear you speak Isako of war rations potatoes one week yellow onions the next mother riddled with stomach pains is like hearing you speak of another life Isako stumbling through streets bolts of silk clutched to your chest begging for handfuls of rice Isako your uncle whispers something about the city bombed like ash your sister and her two girls drift back to you on the wind your brother soon follows overhead a haze of memory so many lifetimes Isako together we stand mist breaking into little tendrils and drifting away Isako the world so bright and buzzing with activity it is difficult Isako to remember you at the center an obliterated city explosions of light buildings immediately flattened above the thicket Isako smoke rises from another life Isako the wail of air raid sirens the life you lead Isako not so distant as you may think

Portrait of Isako in Wartime

Ohio, and I imagine her
       walking the train line,
tracks narrowed in the distance.
       Through her soles,
the platform's slats. She feels
       their unevenness
in the flats of her feet. Noon-
       day heat and the wool
of her jacket's itchy.
       She's got a bob, it's 1943
and the war's on. No one
       in the station looks
like her, but everyone's
       looking at her.
No explanation but the one
       in government-issued print.
National Student Relocation
       Council. *Early Release.*
The sentry in his watch-
       tower, barbed-wire fence
and Stars and Stripes flapping
       in the wind. From across
the tracks, a man (here,
       imagination does the work

history's lost) approaches, finger
            bared, a blunt accusation.
Aren't you a *Jap?* The long
            explanation—why she's out,
whose side she's on.
            The nations we pledge
at odds, leaving us to make
            up the difference.
This story's old, the woman
            —dead, papers boxed
in a back closet. I've seen them.
            Early Release.
The government-issued ID number.

            In camp, it's said, they cut
gardens into Arkansas desert,
            fixed rocks into the flat face
of the earth and irrigated
            bean rows to feed their families.
Healthy vines appeared
            where none should have
grown; tiny buds coaxed
            from the earth, tendrils
that spooled runners
            through dust.

When the order came
        to pack up and return
home, the authorities found
        every curtain drawn
shut. Every barrack
        floor swept clean.

Sunday in Skagit Valley

and you're taking me to see the tulips. But there *are* no tulips.
There! but those are daffodils, crimped trumpets hailing

gaily along the highway. *There!* but those are dandelions,
dressed in delicate lace. On Caledonia, we walk and gawk

at clay chickens cast in copper kettles, ceramic gloves, wrists overrun
with ranunculus and ferns. *There!* Many-hued teacups, hung

from the spokes of a wind vane. *There!* Yellow-throated pansies,
fresh as if just finished. In the Gift & Gallery Shoppe, a vase

like a melted breast, nipple hardened to a point.
Is this a local *artist?* you ask, the Gift & Gallery way

of saying: Is this farm-fresh free-range free-trade chicken?
Actually, the Shoppekeeper says, *it's from* Thai*land.*

You point to me: She *grew up in Thailand.* The Shoppekeeper turns
to look, thinking of her four-day cruise down the Chao Phraya,

the elephant rides and long-necked ladies who kept calling,
calling to each other. Under the gaze of Jungle Fowl ($138),

Winged Fowl ($118), and Dodo Bird ($98), I press my palms together,
an old gesture from my childhood of steepled fingers, bowed heads,

chicken chasing, and that glorious afternoon when I caught one
streaking past, held it high as it *chook-chook-chooked* in conquered

chicken-speak, unwieldy wings flexed in upside-down flight. *Sawadti ka!*
the Shoppekeeper calls, and a blast of bells wrangles into the street.

The Street Where a Certain Democratic Leader Lives

I.

Everywhere the sound of brass tongues breaking against bells and the delicate scent of frangipani. Women with cheeks like acrid moons smeared with yellow paste. Every house shadowed by the heavy gold of the pagoda whose spires spindle into blue. The oily glare of the stupa. A series of unmarked buildings built without windows to make a point of the walls. Inside are women who brush each other's hair to a fine gloss. Around the front gather a group of foreigners trying to make a border. Facing the one-way glass they see only their reflection mirrored both ways. Who is behind the door. Possibly they are chained to a bed or being beaten. Possibly they are bent over a washbasin wringing out their hair. In their nostrils lingers the smell of devil's dung also called hing and ting. Fear is a hallway with no doors. An impossible black that absorbs all light. I look into its lustrous glaze and watch my likeness warp as though pushed through heavy water. In protest I cross the country. At the border I create an edge and apply a distant pressure. Upon arriving the women's arms are pinned above their heads like insect specimens on display. Their arches lift through the pretense of cut glass spread across the floor. If the back is a bridge there must be a way to cross it. Arranged in unnatural configurations the body evokes what some call desire and travel long distances to satisfy. *Hello you like girls* is both question and statement. Am I a part of this. If this is my body then are these its parts. A bottle breaks on a distant counter making a jagged edge.

II.

The street where women are marked and made to stand in a line which makes a border. *Border:* an *edge, a fixed line that cannot be crossed* though the body is flexible and made to perform unnatural acts. Standing there every body tells itself: *I is invisible. I does not exist.* Every body a ragged edge that tells itself *there is no tear* then passes directly through. Labia. Lips. White fabric fluoresces in blacklight. Visible but not. Am I a part of this. Ping-pong ball. Crotch. In the street a woman calls out but there is a blank where her mouth should be.

III.

I emerges from the river with a single piercing in her lip. In time her skin loses its sheen and becomes a sheath seamlessly fit to the body. I is woken frequently by the need to pass through water. In the supple whip of her spine I senses she was once contained by another form. But I has no recollection of any moment but the present. There is only current, the sensation of being trapped within a larger body hurtling through time the way an outboard motor cuts through current. I peers through the folds to see what lies on the other side but has failed to preserve memory thus has no desire to return. Across the water I can make out distant shapes, the path toward which she cannot imagine. I knows not to listen to fish who lie and cannot be trusted.

Cebu

Dusk, my friend and I scrambled
      to shore, slick with
Camotes seawater, as fishermen
      dragged in their nets.
Spread before us, the hem
      of her mother's fishing village;
south, the Celebes Sea.
      Girls! girls! our mothers'
voices, thinned by distance.
      Who heard first, her
or me—and did it matter
      how near the net was?
We held out our hands
      as men filled them
with minnows: violent, silvery
      flashes in the palm.
We swallowed them whole
      and watched the tide
haul in, drank water from
      coconuts—*Like this,* she said,
lifted the split hull to her lips,
      tipped back to catch
the sharp, milky flood.

Running home that night, we wove
        through empty marketplace,
past bitter melon, Malabar spinach,
        past *there,* in a corner
a man holding what appeared—
        through clots of sluggish air,
a limp tuber in his hand,
        fist working back
and forth in the patchy dark,
        shadows bunched around
his slacks' opening. Sallow
        light sucked into eyeholes,
mouth. Face an empty leer.
        A glimpse so quick—did she?
could she? from where she stood—
        caught as we flew
through the last arch
        into family gate.

I couldn't breathe,
        felt the bite of too-tight
bathing suit in armpits
        where the clingy
fabric had worn thin,
        cinched into the surprise

of my body. That night
        I lay in bed, flickering
in, out—the horror of it
        slid through
as beyond, waves pulled
        tight across shore.

After Hiroshima

It took four days to cry
and then—   there was nothing left to say

They say it rained black,
that boys with mouths *swelled to pomegranates*
                drank the water and died—
sick with silt,
                flayed by fire

The skin of a woman's hand
                came away in a medic's grip
mizu   mizu   mizu
                she screamed
knowing water would make her die

In the museum, singed bits of hair,
        a scorched kimono,
                        pink flowers still visible,
charred lunchbox, rice turned to powder,
        stacks of porcelain teacups, fused
                in the   *blinding flash*

O mother   O land
O country   covered in ash,

faces crisped
by fourth-degree burns

blackening or charring of the skin, leathery texture
loss   of all feeling–

To orient:
to face or turn east, to discover
one's position
in relation to another

Standing in the shadow
of the A-Bomb Memorial,
birds dart overhead   in and out
of skeletal frame,
scabbed brick interior crushed,
gutted by fire

Sing to me, Isako,
over your kari rice, pink rollers in your hair
tell me again

–first time I hear god's voice
is over the radio   (to the government
can you imagine?   of the United States
can you   our empire accepts
provisions of declaration   )

To reorient:

> *to align oneself*
>
> *after a disorientation, to undergo a change*
>
> *in essence; to lose*
>
> *one's original nature*

Years later, a woman's body

drifts back into the bay   splits red

when opened

stomach curried with a wire brush—

Polytrauma

(with inscriptions from a painting by Ned Broderick)

begins with a blast, the body filled with foreign fragments

        shred bone and nerve tissue / *frontal cranial eminence missing*

     with corresponding cerebral tissue (6 cm) / 63% coalition fatalities

caused by commercially-sourced explosives / cluster bombs, clothes soaked

        in napalm / soda cans wired into daisy chains

     shrapnel in left temporal area lodged in frontal lobe

desert blast / that *ping-ping-ping* / *left arm mostly torn off* / palms

        massive flesh wound to left side of neck / soldiers held together

     by shoelaces / the Screaming Eagles / *die motherfuckers*

die / the saw's thin whine / *exoneration of left occipital orbit* / sternum

        split / surgeon up to his elbows / *RT external border above clavicle*

     sand fleas / festering wounds / *why do my feet feel so cold*

blood-caked sand / *kill me* / *kill me now* / in the hospital

        body packed back in / *tell me* / sewn shut

     it returns to being / body / tube-stuck pharynx / raw

in the mind / *head injury struck by tank* / a pattern that sets and stays / something

        about them shooting at you / *fragments from hostile device*

     noted in chest cavity / you shooting at them / puts the nerve endings

outside the body / *puncture wound from 50 cal. shell entering left trapezius*

        like mad dogs about to die / trained to hit the gas

     if someone approaches the vehicle / *stop right there!* / clouds of chlorine

woman carrying a white flag / *lodged into left anterior*

frontal lobe / the woman steps / the shot / scream
crunch tires split / skull / *surrounding tissue destroyed*

convoy strung across the berm / tire treads / the pattern set
glistens / blood-streaked trail / *tell me* / white
of flag / red of woman / truth that spreads / dark stain
on asphalt / *tell me I'm gonna be whole again* / pattern bit into skin / rubber teeth
that fix and will not let go / we came in droves / shiny orbs
enemies they can't see / neat O of the muzzles / mad dogs
about to die / white teeth / chewing mouthparts / *Dragon Skin*
can't close your eyes / can't close your ears

tell me / *die*

Legion My Lesion

oh adamantine jaw light
to limb oh bloat come
halo red gummed block

when was your last
meal have you eaten
drunk anything male

consent would you like
to keep your belongings
race gender creed height

eye tick hours drip tubing
wire sick mouth wrench
gum pry peel suture hew

hem lip place slide pound
scab sore split flake ache
softened reddening gums

choke throat cavity
handbells radiance leg
shanks a rank bloom

Portrait in Sickness and Health

A mechanical beeping fills the space around your bed. Without warning there is a jerking and tongue fluttering followed by a grayness that sets in. Your tongue flattens making a croaking sound as the eyes whiten in the head. When I tell the nurse in the next cubicle *please can you come* what I say has a gray and sickly shine. Is plugged with needles and cannot leave the building.

As you are wheeled through the double doors I hear a mouth ripping which is mine. One of me kisses when the nurse says kiss but the other disappears through the nearest exit. Is it possible the body on the gurney is the same as the bare skin and shoulders beside me in bed this morning.

One of me sits in a room counting the houndstooth on the chair in front of me. Another stands in the hallway watching the doors open and close. There is the sound of someone snoring. Across the room a woman touches her eyes with a tissue. The doors swing around empty air. The nurses have gone through and so have you. When I see you again it will be with a different face.

Recovery

Behind a white curtain, the family gathers close— me   your parents   sisters

Against a scrim of wires, lights blip incoherently
        monitoring your body—   breached   bruised

The nurse hooks a bladder to the stand over your bed, shows you
        how to operate the up/down function, the call button's fat "t"—

an "x" with a foreshortened leg   fixed to the arm of the bed

its grim plastic frame   center a motorized hinge
        a drawn-up knee   padded with sheets

Blue flowers on your cotton shift   white piping around the armholes,
        collar widened for head   swelled cheeks

Beyond the curtain, another family   outline of their bodies against fabric
        swells, dissolves

A lattice of tubing hooked from the ceiling   clear liquid slides

drip by drip through rubber vein   O afterlife   O instant breakfast tray
          O styrofoam cup of apple juice

If you need anything   the doctor   the nurse

Behind the curtain, we speak in voices hushed by   sound of TV applause
          synthesizers   occasional cymbals
                                                  Can you move your lips
The stiffness of hospital behavior
          You're looking fabulous   *recovering beautifully*

what's wheeled through hallways   funneled down elevators

Before touching the body   every nurse snaps latex gloves onto fingers
          pulls the wrinkles out before handling

A notched screwdriver turns in the fleshy incision
          of your cheek   sutured shut

We leave you   blue from the light of the television

the slow squeeze   of saline above your bed

the heart's bright jerky lunge across the screen   cross
          the threshold   press the door

listen for the latch to stutter across the plate   wait
        for it to find its way

inside   you clasp and unclasp the blue-flowered hinge of your body

Crossing

Driving home in the close heat
        of brittle hair & seat leather,
I work my hand into your hold,
        tell you about buried head-
waters, narrow feet, and that great
        meandering belly whose waters
hold us all: giant ibis, sarus crane.
        Against the tick of sidewalk grid
I recall that water, its shift and glimmer,
        the scaly creatures that lurk in delta
only crossable—in those days—by ferry.
        Back then, I edged sideways
down chipped steps to keep
        from falling, lived bounded
by the other shore, fed off its muddy vein.
        Rice paddies heaped in wide terraces,
river slopes dotted with broad-backed buffalo
        crusted in mud. Those days, life
lurched from dock to deck, pitched by armpits
        toward the opposite bank.

Later you hold me close, our bodies
        tacky with sweat. *I thought*
I'd fall, I whisper, work a slow eddy

against your bank. Overhead,
the fan turns a hypnotic swirl. Our darks
rise. Silver currents of carp,
catfish. *I'm afraid.* A misplaced foot
and I'm lost to the wild seam
of water between dock and hull,
fallen to bits between
thrashing blades— overhead,
the roar of outboard motor
and sound of loose flip-flops across deck.
I'm scared I'll be left behind,
churned alone in this dark
whiskery mouth, as on deck,
you're lost in the squeal of split
tires on boat edge.
In the sticky heat, you reach all the way
around. *Hold me,* I say
and disappear in the water's strangeness,
its gritty shift against skin.

Part II:
A History
of Lost Things

Late Pantoum: Isako, Illness

You wake to the rattle of porcelain
against rim, turn to unhappy linens:
rumpled pillow, cast-off duvet. Mouth
steeped in bitters, you rise to clear

the bedroom of unhappy linens,
breakfast things: butter pat, tea cozy
steeped in bitters. You rise, clear
the mug with the chipped lip

and other breakfast things. Left
to the cozy tyranny of drying rack,
the mug with the chipped lip
whispers mutiny along its ceramic edge.

The tyranny of the dying wracks
the china saucer, whose cracked
ceramic rim whispers: *Mutiny.*
Silver clamors in the hall cabinet

where china saucers crack and brim
with rumpled silverfish. Their velvet
mouths clamor in the hall cabinet
for your wake, upsetting the porcelain.

Garden Song

Knives. Your children are coming to dinner
all clamor and grab, faces ticking with greed
like teeth left fastened too long in the head.

Left untended, your mind's gone maggoty,
rotted like the cold center of a plum. Hungry
in the head, rows of unpolished spoons, knives.

They've hired a woman to haunt the hallway,
fetch the bone china. Left as a tribulation
when you die, the chard will run rampant.

Unhemmed, the bean rows will loosen
like old muscles in the mouth, come
undone in the garden's thistled heart.

Sakai Bros. Nursery

(in memorium)

in the twilight   era of the family

     the nursery lies in ruins

busted steel rafters   a flattened ghetto of glass

     panes cracked and missing

     a face with the teeth blown out

what do I call this   place harvested of memory

     the house where Isako was born

steps built after the war   *Demolition Pending*

     thorns bristle like hair on the nape

floribundas gape against glass   a blaze of eyes

     is it possible   to be empty and brimming

     at the same time

57

Elegy for the Unborn

Little *are-you-there*,
seen-through body   touched by a pulse so faint
it's a glow about the chest

—are you there?

I've a sadness   I say
a callous nest of ligament
in the scooped-out shallow
of my hipbone.

A sadness
little rows of buttons   pressed powder faces
—lines for noses, curly skritches for eyes
crushed between molars,
fine dust left on lips   left
oh little where-
have-you-gone—

where have you gone?

Pressed to silt   dust
this time for mourning

not gladness but weeping
my chest cavity withers.
Sealed eyes rattle in plastic pockets

pop   pop-pop
foil split from backing—rows

pink & pink & pink

      &   a row of white.
A pale watery streak

               left *where*– oh *where*
oh little barely-

                    there   you were never

                                  there.

          A time *for casting*
for gathering   fingers so thin,

                 a radiance around the wrist.

Three Scenes from the Body

(Seattle, Santa Barbara, etc.)

I.

Here is the kettle; here is the cold bowl of rice

Here at midnight is the kettle's nose song, the *brrrrrrz* of the microwave
       whirling rice in its square plastic belly

white door   white counter   rows of white tile stained with old grout and spaghetti—
       I am alone here   —bright light reflects off the tabletop

the face of the clock *chuck-chocks* loudly on the yellow wall

Finish your snack   Come back to bed

Oh! You are creaking down the hallway, closer and closer

I stare at the light coming off the counters the tips of my fingers
       into rice bowl

There is sleep in your eye   in the bright topiary of my mind
       I hide and hide   *Come back to bed.*

Into the soft pink hole of my mouth I shovel and shovel this watery concoction
       seaweed   home   tea broth   rice   mothersalt

When it comes to the end I use my fingers

I in my underpants   nightdress billowing like a parachute
                into the rafters   I rise and rise

                                        Come back to bed

II.

carved like a back risen spine-like shell over coral sheets something sinister seeps starfish creep fingerpull by fingerpull inch by scabbed crustacean inch walls alive eyes cracked wallseam lit from lamp domed scallop set in ceiling who hides beneath headboard clatters beneath bed rush of shower here is only you and shadow blended cream of wall shook free of suck lips loosed from cling centers cracked like hinge of oyster shucked clean of meat I crawl jagged limbs of me of fingers clatter inch up bedstream into the shoal of you crabbed banks stitched pearl white mother of pearl lover fish flower face stranger coarse laughter strings of pearl sticky pearls drip flower drip

III.

In this city of mist and salted fish,
morning spreads as thin as pale

margarine on toast. Light dims in
the sky, retreats like a rueful child

returned too soon to bed. Fixed
in the gaze of an opaque eye, we

huddle in fog, edges eroded
by shadow and steam *(shoulder, neck bone)*.

Love, think of the salmon laid in shiny strips
along the shore, gutting themselves

muscle on muscle on water on rock—
breached, beating themselves to bits.

Isako Cries after the Wedding

Because in the mirror your face glows
with a plastic sheen. Because your lips
are a perfect bud, and the curve of your arm
is a long-stemmed brush plied high across
your cheek. Because you look nothing like
yourself, and the tassel of the potted plant
hanging beside your head isn't what
you imagined when you imagined this day.
Because you've done this a thousand times,
woken from sweat to blush your cheeks,
ready your hair. Because like your dreams,
the eyebrows you pluck tighten like traces
across your forehead. Because your breasts
cupped in his hands feel heavy, ache.

The Sister Watches the Recessional

Being dead, I couldn't see their faces,
but knew from the way people let fly
handfuls of birdseed, this was a day
to celebrate. From the way she turned
into his suit, how her skirt twisted and ran
to its train, I knew it was a happy occasion.
I saw her duck as she passed, shield
her face with carnations and roses.
Everybody cheered but me. Light blanched
sections of her dress, the right side of his chest,
the crease in his hair where he'd parted it
down the center. I watched her veil froth
and foam, rise around her face. *Turn around,*
I wanted to shout. *I'm in the eaves.*

At the Cliff House

(San Francisco)

Hedge grass, juniper. The cliff bares
its back teeth. Stone-faced, you slip
a black knot over your wrists, fuse

the ends with flame. How many times
have you stopped short, breath
jerked from the throat? To lose

yourself in the fall; to have lost it all
to need, affliction. Crank the heart's
ugly lever, set this machine back

into motion. The bronze star points
north but never resolves. North-northwest,
east-northeast. May you find your way

by its burnished light. Here, take this
talisman of good faith. A handful of
broken rocks, bullets for the journey.

Isako Shows Her Daughter How to Ply the Line

How to work the barb into the throat. Reaching after the hook

she scrapes her finger on a line of teeth.   The lake's surface flares.
        She cuts away from the tail, along the lateral.

There are many ways to gut a fish. White flesh falls open   unzipped
        at the seam.

The child refuses the rod, will not take barb or bait. The line hangs
        empty.

Lake smooth & undisturbed   a mirror without a face.

What peers from the belly   a kind of betrayal. How many lives does it take
        to satisfy a line, a limit.

What we see in the face of the mirror
        what prevents us from dipping our own into it.

The landed body flips and shivers. Pulled onto sandy bank
        gills gape like terrible wounds—

air drawn from the body   *a cut, a whistle.*

When does the leaving occur   skin stiff as chain mail. Rigor mortis.

To debone a fish, lift the tail and scrape the scales forward. Loosen the flesh
        until it pulls free.

Unfold the ribs' feathery architecture, then flip and repeat. Lay the halves
        side by side   as imperfect mirrors.

In the child's body, a growing sleekness. The skin thins and repels
        rain. Scales develop.

Cut the line, the child says   showing her affinity for fish. What fails to pass
        from one set of hands

to the next. What slips away   trailing a cut line. Netting a fish proves harder
        than it looks.

Isako fears her line has run to its end. The departed body
        fills with radiance.

There is no way to know if a fish is female if you refuse to split the hull.

Pity the Child

Pity the girl
child asleep

in the back
room, lying

among her dolls,
toy kitchen. Tea-

cups, colander—
light draining

from the room
as she sleeps.

How the walls
thicken. Her

unsuspecting form,
every shadow

making its way
toward her.

The Kind of Morning

(Vietnam War Memorial)

The kind of morning a plane could lift into from runway and   disappear
        swallowed by fog: wing tip, cockpit.

The kind of morning that clings to face   coat   wet seams of umbrella
        nylon spread like surrender across

ribs, which in this tamped-down light appear skeletal. What we don't see

up top, a snub-nosed bomb dropped into jungle   disappears the minute it's released

swallowed by jungle canopy   ropy vines.

A child runs screaming   trails shreds of skin   white
        feet bare.

Names start at the ankle.   Mist gathers in ghost patterns—
        looking down I see tennis shoes, notched rubber soles.

How sleek, invisible the undergrowth

swift multiplicity of black granite pushing against itself, pressed into earth
        feet step independent of volition

faces made flat   shiny   pressed into stone.

Harsh geese overhead   mistaken for gulls, firebirds
          (no we've not forgotten)

what mistaken for silence becomes a fall, a slide without side rails

each step notched into the next widening, stacking granite higher
          above the head   and heavier.

Atop the head there's a blue of sorts   but I see only gray
          fog that clings, will not let go

that mistaken for names   (*propagates* is the word) swiftly replicates itself
          widens then splits.

Breathing's difficult now. The constriction of apex, its terrible reach, spectacle seamed
          black on black

made ghosts, made echoes, made a red plastic geranium crimped in half
          draggled in gravel

a sore remnant.

Rain runs fingers through names.   Like all good men, keeps accounts from the house
          there on the hill   what you see once lifted from the pit

slatted runway into air, up top where breathing's easier, where color's turned back.

Up steps up pillars   behind the white lattice, Mr. Lincoln in his counting house
          eating bread and honey.

Granite seeps from sight as through a sieve
        gashes in vision sucking it past in pieces, splinters

the sign for a man whose name begins with a cross
        circled off   a closed circuit   pricked as if by the point of a knife.

Snow crunches   under foot   again the grackle of geese.

Isako's Rules to Remember

You will be sent for by mail and arrive by ship. Shocking pink is a fine color to wear. To travel in style is the only way. A daughter-in-law is like a servant without a wage. Your mother will arrive by plane with feet swollen in her new shoes. The daughter you bear will neither speak your language nor understand your customs. Your granddaughter: even worse. *Monday. Wednesday. Tuesday. How are you. Go away from here.* You will help your mother copy these phrases into a small black notebook and one day you will find her marching in a parade at the county fair. With this you will learn there is more than one way to make a way.

Lost Things I

Isako keeps careful chronicle of lost things. Mother. Father. Hairpin. During war Isako loses city which is also now. Always some nation under foreign attack. Air raid sirens. Busted brick and shrapnel. *Isako's History of Lost Things.* Line after line of persons lost or missing. Photographs of Isako as child. As bride shrouded in high-toned luxury. Not to mention silk kimono and Meiji castle. Most importantly daughter from first marriage only discovered years later. Confession recalled on family scroll also lost. After second marriage Isako scrapes rice from bamboo rice bowl rinsed with tea broth. *Look what's become of you.* Silver gelatin prints from Isako's previous life. What she calls a mystery. How can a life be lost if it was never yours.

Isako Recalls Her Father's Death

As Isako tells it, upon entering the house, her mother moves as if to close the gaping mouth but instead pulls a white handkerchief from her sleeve, which placed over the father's face becomes a mask. In death, the body a voided form. A soul swept clean. As Isako tells it, her mother covers the corpse with silk, and there's a glimpse of purple tongue, visible then veiled. Isako recalls her mother's voice, a sudden coldness in the stomach. They bear the burden in the dark, feet slipping in mud. Along the river a path extends, a question with no end. An ache begins in Isako's hands, moves to her chest. How a door torn from its hinge becomes a pall. The body, a form through which we pass.

Lost Things II

Speaking of Isako I lose my place. Who is Isako. I flip through family photos as Isako recalls her life. Isako is mother seated beside child in cowboy hat blowing birthday candles. Is somber child in geta peeking from hem of kimono. Is 1933. 1956. Is figure proliferated through time. I need some record to keep Isako fixed in place. To chronicle deaths births important dates. The family scroll where is it. Again I lose my place. In this chronicle of Isako's life no beginning or end only a set of faces unfolding endlessly. Yet Isako remembers every detail. Street songs from childhood. The trolley bell's *chin chin chin*. Her daughter's lip split on the corner of the coffee table. Please. Recount to Isako your own anecdotes and discover if she too remembers.

Isako, Last Spring

Isako Isako have you run to your end.

Isako Isako is there an end and if so is it near.

Isako Isako will I see you again.

Isako Isako you are mostly bone. My hand on your spine as you lower onto the white couch.

Isako Isako I turn the pages of your life and find you on every spread. Eyes solemn beneath schoolgirl bangs. Foot turned to accentuate the line of your body. An Isako for every age.

Isako Isako I bring you a Kleenex. I clip a hangnail and file the edges smooth.

Isako Isako I want so badly to smooth the hair from your forehead.

The way my daughter likes it when I sing her to sleep.

Isako Isako you have so many faces.

Isako Isako if I could reach out and touch one it would be enough.

Isako Isako if I could take your words in my mouth. Press your cheek to mine and watch the skin dissolve.

Isako Isako outside your window the cherry tree is in full bloom.

Every branch lit with pink blossoms. A riot of renewed life.

Isako Isako when I see you again it will be with a different face.

Isako Isako you reach through time to take my hand.

Isako Isako yours is such a small hand.

Isako Isako the air in the room suddenly stirred. My hand clasped in your lap.

Isako Isako my hands now brim with you.

Isako Isako this page my hands this voice your breath.

Isako Isako I can see it now.

Isako Isako there is no end.

Isako Isako I is you.

Part III:
In the Quiet
after

The Losing Begins

(for Isako, at last)

Long before you're gone, the losing begins.
And slow. And slow. You let go in inches,
starting with the shoulders, the ulna, wrist,
until each hand is rung with light. I never
imagined it this way. How the body goes
in stages. And the mind, leeched through
a crack at the base of the skull. No name
for this, though it's the word that makes it
bearable. The edge, blunted. Run, I will
run from this. The world caws brightly,
the crown of my head bursts with youth.
Yet this is how it ends. Who will bear this
dark shard in the eye, that the end when
it comes, dresses us down without mercy?
Small wonder, the racket you made at
the child's approach. Ha—*ha!* To skeletal
teeth in head, bared. To flat hands, palms
clapped bone against bone, *thwack thwack,*
warding off demons as they gather like grim
congregants around your bed. This strange
anointing. This new spirit. How we fend.

Salmon Song: Migration

(Chittenden Locks, Seattle)

You throw the whole of your
      weight into this. You, against

me, driving into the beyond,
      pushing through murky green,

bodies glinting like some ancient,
      battered foil. Up and in

to spawn, to die. Back to
      the originating impulse.

You tunnel onward, reptilian,
      lit by a bluish glow,

tight-laid scales a rainbow
      hatching across the flank.

I imagine you caught, cored.
      Bodies spread like shattered

silver across the dock.
      Not that I will it, though

your restless form impels
       against the drag of mine,

the whole of me against
       the whole of you, flayed

bodies pressing on,
       up weirs and rapids,

arrowed by impossible force.

Bathing Isako

At the end she mostly slept, had little to say.
We swabbed her skin to fend off fever, but
still her tongue cracked like old leather.
Her lips peeled, hips thinned. Her legs,
shrunk in their sockets, turned to baggy
flesh-colored stockings. We cut a slit
in her nightgown: pink, puffed sleeves,
washed and returned her to sleep.

The afternoon she died, she was lying
on her side when, from beyond the frame
of body and bedside, a glow bathed her
skin with an uncanny luster. Sprays of light
from the cut face of her wedding ring,
gold flecks spinning across the ceiling.

What I remember: her eyes opening,
blue-gray and rheumy with wonder.
Ah! she said, like a child, pointing
at the wild inflections of light leaping
harum-scarum across the room. *Look!*
she said, hands flying—and again, *look!*

Departure

I felt the room go cold when she died,
looked at her lying there, thought, *how still
she seems.* How smooth, like time had erased
the particularity from her face, worked
some strange alchemy to make her less
of herself, more like the women I'd seen
in black-and-white portraits on the mantel,
stoic immigrant faces from another time.

There was her body, and then it was just
a body. I wasn't there for the cremation—
they put her remains in a cardboard box,
passed it slowly through an incinerator
as the family stood behind a glass wall.
They say they watched until the flames
were through. That after the burning,
there was nothing left to see.

I once lost my way home from school,
crossed mistakenly through temple
grounds and found myself in the middle
of a funeral. Greasy smoke, the scent
of scorched hair and skin that clung
to my clothes. The whole village, wailing,

gathered around the stink of burnt flesh,
and in the center, a dark shape that spat
and blackened on the pyre, glowed
white-hot, and then burst to ash.

In the Quiet after

I.

Body still. Pulse thinned to a thready tic,
all that remains. Sore-split tongue, worn
skin, sunk limbs attached to hips. Lids, low.
Below the lashes; a dim, rheumy line.

What remains—sores on the tongue, split.
The body, cradled in the palm of the bed
—*dust to ashes*. The dim, rheumy eyelids,
mouth pried open by some unholy force.

The body, an offering—a cradle of bones.
Breath drags from the throat, a rusted chain
in the mouth. Some unknown face marks
the children with the names of the dead.

Breath drags through the throat. Rusty chains
pour down the spine, rise in the mind
of the children. The names of the dead,
like life, hang on a finely balanced line.

Fear pulls at the mind, rises in the spine,
body. Pulse stills. Thinned to a thready tic,
life hangs upon a finely balanced line.
Limbs detach from hips, lift from skin.

II.

I searched every box, pried lids open like oysters,
after some indeterminate thing. Old lipstick,

safety pins, a man's gold watch. In the bottom drawer,
a stack of old photos. A boy holds a trout, a girl waves

from the inside of an Oldsmobile. That's her,
in sunglasses and a silk neckerchief on the steps

of the Acropolis. Her again, laughing
in the packing shed. The room fills with roses.

A man wears suspenders, an unfamiliar face.
Baby teeth, a clamshell. In a gilt-edged case,

an old ring set with luminous eyes.
The drawer slides shut. Her smile braces

against the lens. One of the gems is cracked
through the center: a jealous eye. Someone

tells the story. Someone covers their face.
Grief settles like a fine red silt.

III.

When she had just started being dead,
I reached for her hand, stroked it. Worked
the tough red skin in circles until blood rose
to the surface. Veins crept green across
the radial, into the network of the palm.

When she had been dead a while, the roses
drying by her bedside crimpled like paper.
I left them there—missing the smell of her,
it seemed the thing to do. Heads split
from brittle stems, a cascade
of dried petals tossed in air.

IV.

From the bed she rises, steals through rooms
after things she cannot bring: sterling silver,
Noritake china, strings of freshwater pearls
hung in toothy grins. She tidies the soul's affairs:
shakes out rugs, scrapes grime from windowsills.
The night comes unmoored. She trims toenails
grown long and painted, pinches cold cheeks,
eases the throat's gauntlet, snaps her teeth shut
like the lips of a coin purse—and, before leaving,
tapes a spare key to the mouth of the drain.

One Day You'll Look in the Mirror and See Lions

May you not fear what lies ahead.
       May the moon's full face
              light your own, milky
with tears. May it ferry you into mystery.
       May your body, luminous
              in its skin, so thin the bones
                    glow through, brim
              with whispered prayers,
lacrimal and lesser wings.

May the lion's mouth be shut.
       May its head sink to the ground
              at your approach, splendid
       in your cotton nightie, an apparition
of joint and socket plainly revealed.
       May you stand and be spared.
              Please, all I ask.

Cast in greenish light, your hands rise,
       tendril-like, to receive
              a fullness your daughter,
       drawing near, feels spilling
onto her fingers. Poor soul, you can see
              the fear lifting like smoke

off her skin. *Don't fight*, you want to say.
Come, stroke the beast's shaggy head.

    Pull open its terrible maw, see

        for yourself, not the teeth

    you expect, but the gentle rumination
of bovid incisors, muted tongue.

    Come, child. Lie with the lion.

      The ox, the lamb.

A Last History of Isako

Isako is lady with split shears under bed in case of emergency. Is lady
knot red wool through thumb bow. Is lady thrust fist and shank

                                      into dark   cutting edge first.

                    Is still. Is viscera   pressed into body. Is waiting.
Is time. Is breath grated against teeth

                                    like heavy object dragged over
chain link. Is jaw wrenched open.

                         Isako is lady. Is not.   Is Toyo

                is Lois is Sachiko is Shigeko is
Is body. Is passed through incinerator in cardboard box. Is witnessed
by family who waits until flames are through.

                            Is lady. Is ash. Is air.

                    Is feet is memory is skin is

Without Isako there is only the present moment which folds into a bright star lodged in the eye.

Without Isako I have nothing to say.

I sit before a page voided of language.

I drink my tea.

I fold my hands and place my head on my palms.

I hear the door click shut as someone leaves the room.

I close my eyes and listen hard.

I hear nothing but the breath whistling in the back of my throat.

I feel nothing but the vice on my temples.

Without Isako the body is a foreign land with no way into its secrets. The mind that will not clear, the jaw that buckles in the mouth.

I fill with buzzing light refracted off the present moment. Its impenetrable architecture and hard reflective surfaces.

Without Isako there is no way to move through.

I stumble down unfamiliar streets in a haze of forgetting.

Have I been here before?

Names loosen from faces and disappear in a labyrinth of memory.

Where is Isako. Who is Isako. Are you Isako.

Will you help me remember what I have forgotten.

Balloon Bombs

(Bly, Oregon, 1945)

What the children saw,

        hiking up Gearhart Mountain—

what they thought was a weather balloon

            snagged in a stand of ponderosa.

      They hadn't heard the radio reports:

                Any balloon found   *approaching our borders*

                      may be an enemy attack.

      Wayward bombs caught on fences, telephone poles—

                   mysterious explosions   fires.

      I watched the documentary

            in a church basement   folding chair, Styrofoam coffee cup.

             How did they make the crossing?

            Baffled experts handle ballast bags

                   the size of a child's fist.

            The younger sister asks—   *Is Dick dead?*

                   And Sis?

    The reel snags   frames flip and slow

        image blurred   ghostly   shroud lines

            disappear into distance.

        Schoolgirls in white collars, pleated skirts   pound washi

to pulp, work it to a wet slurry. Soldiers march an ugly goose step

      around the city, bristling with bayonets.

        Tokyo leveled   debris like blown paper.

Something terrible has happened.

An eye-stabbing flash   cinders blot out the sun
searing heat   flesh tears   turns to charcoal
girls' foreheads bound with strips of cotton   streaks
across a grainy screen.
Peel the skin off in sheets
stitch the panels together   press with konnyaku glue.

After the explosion, they staggered home,
skin stained yellow from picric acid.
Seared limbs, picnic clothes.

The lights flicker on.
What is it we wish for? Vengeance,
forgiveness. Prayers for what we, in the shadow
of the Mitchell Memorial, call healing.
Silence is security.
Yame schoolgirls fold cranes, wish for peace.
I've tried this from every angle.

The soldier in the sentry tower   rifle slung over his shoulder,
a boy in uniform made to stand attention   over Modoc
desert endless through his cross hairs.
Grit gathers in his throat   every day he swallows harder.

The sister, hiding under the back seat
of a locked car. In the kitchen, her mother trails

97

a telephone cord, voice high as helium.   What she wishes—
                              to bomb the internment camp   sixty miles away
                                                    blast the last barrack to ash.

The man interned at Tule Lake   who wakes every morning
                         to the scrape of steel shovels,   the sound of his neighbor's wife
          snapping wet shirts on the porch.   *Ditches to dig, barracks to build.*
                    He's got family in Hiroshima,
                              watches the sun set   on two horizons.

Distended bellies hang low with bags of sand
          cities flatten   rivers swarm with bodies.
What we pray for   bodies that burst to flame
          mouths that split and swell   kamikaze wind visited
on our enemies   those across the sea   behind barbed wire
                         let them turn   to dust
                    let them   O
                                        god   let them.

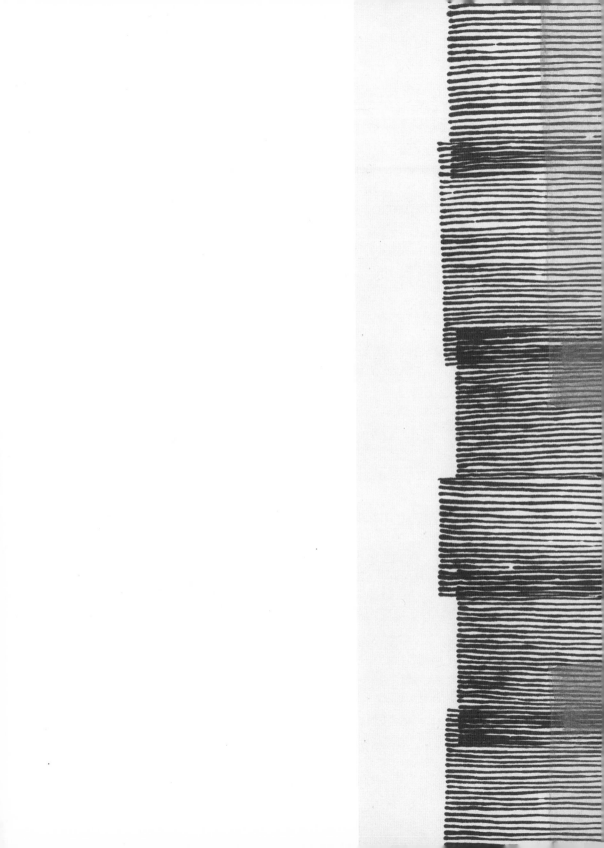

Notes

The epigraph is from Naomi Ruth Lowinsky's *The Motherline: Every Woman's Journey to Find Her Female Roots* (Fisher King Press, 1992).

"To My Many Mothers, Issei and Nisei" is after a poem by Patricia Smith.

The document after the opening poem is a facsimile of Civilian Exclusion Order No. 34, posted after the bombing of Pearl Harbor to enact President Roosevelt's Executive Order 9066.

"As If" is derived from Ezekiel 16:4-12.

"Self-Portrait as Sparrows and Blood" describes a Jewish sacrificial practice detailed in Leviticus 14:4-6. The sparrows alluded to in the opening line of the poem are a part of a Buddhist merit-making ceremony.

"City of Sandalwood" refers to the Pali name of Vientiane, the capital city of Laos.

"After Hiroshima" includes details from the Mayo Clinic's "Burns: Symptoms" (www.mayoclinic.org), Dictionary.com, and Yoshiteru Kosakai's *A-Bomb: A City Tells Its Story* (trans. Kiyoko Kageyama, Charlotte Susu-mago, and Kaoru Ogura, Hiroshima Peace Culture Foundation, 1972).

"Polytrauma" contains inscriptions from an untitled painting by Ned Broderick and phrases from the documentary film *Operation Homecoming: Writing the Wartime Experience*, directed by Richard Robbins (The Documentary Group, 2007), and the Wikipedia article "Improvised explosive device."

The third section of "Another History of Isako" was inspired by the exhibit *Art of Another Kind: International Abstraction and the Guggenheim 1949–1960*, which appeared at the Solomon R. Guggenheim Museum from June 8–September 12, 2012.

"Isako Shows the Child How to Ply the Line" contains a phrase inspired by C.D. Wright's *Just Whistle: A Valentine* (Kelsey Street Press, 1993).

The third section of "In the Quiet after" borrows two lines from Brenda Hillman's *Death Tractates* (Wesleyan University Press, 1992).

"Balloon Bombs" is based on images and interviews from the documentary film *On Paper Wings*, produced and directed by Ilana Sol (A Film Is Forever, 2008). Details are also derived from the article "Death by Balloon Bomb" by Stephen Most from The Oregon History Project (www.oregonhistoryproject.org).

Book Benefactors

Alice James Books wishes to thank the following individual(s) who generously contributed toward the publication of *Isako Isako*:

Sudarshan Malhotra

For more information about AJB's book benefactor program, contact us via phone or email, or visit alicejamesbooks.org to see a list of forthcoming titles.

Recent Titles from Alice James Books

Of Marriage, Nicole Cooley

The English Boat, Donald Revell

We, the Almighty Fires, Anna Rose Welch

DiVida, Monica A. Hand

pray me stay eager, Ellen Doré Watson

Some Say the Lark, Jennifer Chang

Calling a Wolf a Wolf, Kaveh Akbar

We're On: A June Jordan Reader, Edited by Christoph Keller and Jan Heller Levi

Daylily Called It a Dangerous Moment, Alessandra Lynch

Surgical Wing, Kristin Robertson

The Blessing of Dark Water, Elizabeth Lyons

Reaper, Jill McDonough

Madwoman, Shara McCallum

Contradictions in the Design, Matthew Olzmann

House of Water, Matthew Nienow

World of Made and Unmade, Jane Mead

Driving without a License, Janine Joseph

The Big Book of Exit Strategies, Jamaal May

play dead, francine j. harris

Thief in the Interior, Phillip B. Williams

Second Empire, Richie Hofmann

Drought-Adapted Vine, Donald Revell

Refuge/es, Michael Broek

O'Nights, Cecily Parks

Yearling, Lo Kwa Mei-en

Sand Opera, Philip Metres

Alice James Books has been publishing poetry since 1973. The press was founded in Boston, Massachusetts as a cooperative wherein authors performed the day-to-day undertakings of the press. This collaborative element remains viable even today, as authors who publish with the press are also invited to become members of the editorial board and participate in editorial decisions at the press. The editorial board selects manuscripts for publication via the press's annual, national competition, the Alice James Award. AJB remains committed to its founders' original mission to support women poets, while expanding upon the scope to include poets of all genders, backgrounds, and stages of their careers. In keeping with our efforts to foster equity and inclusivity in publishing and the literary arts, AJB seeks out poets whose writing possesses the range, depth, and ability to cultivate empathy in our world and to dynamically push against silence. The press was named for Alice James, sister to William and Henry, whose extraordinary gift for writing went unrecognized during her lifetime.

DESIGNED BY
PAMELA A. CONSOLAZIO
Spark
design

Printed by McNaughton & Gunn